Dear Parent:

An important lesson emerges from thi̷
Some people are inclined to make neg̷
about others who look different, and th̷ ̷̷ ̷̷̷̷ wrong.
("It's wrong to judge a creature by its color or its size.")
What's more, such judgments are not supported by the
facts. Clifford's size may be an impediment for success in
some social situations. For instance, it doesn't help him earn
the trust of the mailman or the new neighbors. These people are so intimidated by the big red dog's size that they fail to
see his splendid qualities of loyalty and generosity, and his
eagerness to please.

It turns out, however, that Clifford's size has advantages for
the community. His bigness comes in handy when there is a
fire to put out. No one else could have done such a fine job
during that emergency on Birdwell Island. So rather than
decry differences, we should welcome them, benefit from
them, and learn from them.

*A cautionary word, however:* Often when young children notice
and remark about observed differences in skin color, size,
dress, or custom, their comments are simple observations of
fact which lack the cultural biases of adults. Granted, audible
queries like, "Mommy, why does that man have no arms?" can
be embarrassing, but they are simply innocent expressions of
wonder. Young children haven't yet mastered
the art of polite evasion. They call it as they
see it—another reason why respect for
differences is most effectively taught
to them not by talk, but by genuine
example.

Adele M. Brodkin, Ph.D.

Visit Clifford at scholastic.com/clifford

ISBN 0-439-41191-2

Copyright © 2001 Scholastic Entertainment Inc. All rights reserved.
Based on the CLIFFORD THE BIG RED DOG book series published by Scholastic Inc. TM & © Norman Bridwell. SCHOLASTIC, CARTWHEEL BOOKS, and associated logos are trademarks and/or registered trademarks of Scholastic Inc. CLIFFORD, CLIFFORD THE BIG RED DOG, and associated logos are trademarks and/or registered trademarks of Norman Bridwell.

Library of Congress Cataloging-in-Publication Data is available

10 9 8                    01 02 03 04 05 06

Printed in the U.S.A.   24
First printing, January 2001

# Clifford THE BIG RED DOG®
# Welcome to Birdwell Island

Adapted by Peggy Kahn

Illustrated by Studio Orlando

**Based on the Scholastic book series
"Clifford The Big Red Dog"
by Norman Bridwell**

From the television script
"Welcome to Birdwell Island" by Dev Ross

Cartwheel
·B·O·O·K·S· ®

SCHOLASTIC INC.
New York   Toronto   London   Auckland   Sydney   Mexico City
New Delhi   Hong Kong

Clifford is the sweetest dog

That you will ever see.

I am so very lucky

That he belongs to me.

There's just a little problem

I hope you'll realize.

The problem isn't Clifford.

It's simply Clifford's size.

Cities are crowded and busy.

A dog needs space to run.

We're moving to Birdwell Island.

Clifford, it will be such fun!

Most pets will fit on a ferry.

Some ride inside a canoe.

But Clifford's so large

That we've hired a barge.

And you like it, Clifford.

Don't you?

**Woof! Woof!**

You like it. You like it. You do!

When the ferry reaches shore,

A gangplank is put in place.

A man on the dock says, "Welcome!"

As a smile lights up his face.

My parents leave the boat.

They wait for me on the dock.

As they chat with the friendly workers,

The dock begins to rOck,

               rock,

                  rOck. . . .

The cause of the commotion
Isn't hard to see:
It's big.
    It's red.
        It wags its tail.
            It's Clifford, naturally!

"Yikes!" yell the men on the dock.

"Okay, big dog. WHOA!"

They see that Clifford likes them,

But they're happy to see him go.

My family's glad that our new house

Has a yard on a quiet street.

Here come two neighbors to meet them

With a cake for a welcome treat.

Mom and Dad are smiling.

We all say, "How do you do?"

I ask, "Would you like to meet my dog?"

And call **"Cliffooord!"**

When they say they do.

Out of his doghouse bounds Clifford.

Up in the air flies the cake.

*Whammo!* Look where it's landing!

The shock makes the hose start to shake. . . .

*Swoosh!* Watch the water go streaming.

Uh-oh! Look who's soaking wet!

Did Clifford toss cakes or spray water?

Will Clifford get blamed? Make a bet!

"That huge dog," they say, "is huge trouble."

"That huge dog will be a huge pest."

They don't stop to ask, "Is he friendly?"

They're so sure what they think is best.

Clifford is so disappointed.

He's gentle. He's kind and he's good.

If people would just get to know him,

They'd like him. Don't you think they would?

The mailman is frightened of Clifford.

Then Jetta, whose dog is called Mac,

Says, "Your dog's too big for this island.

Wherever you came from, go back!"

Poor Clifford, don't worry. I love you.

I'll play catch with you every day.

But just as we start playing,

The wind whisks our toy away.

We watch it sail over the rooftops.

We watch it sail over the park.

Clifford is running to get it.

He thinks this game is a lark!

The people from Birdwell Island,

Who have all seen Clifford before,

Cringe when they see him running.

He's simply too big to ignore.

Some of them start complaining:

"He's trouble."

"He slobbers."

But then . . .

The wail of a siren stops them.

The woods are on fire again!

When the people find the fire chief,

He tells them what they can do.

"Our water tank's not big enough,

So it's lucky we've got you.

Fill those buckets at the pond.

Form a long line and then. . .

Pass those buckets down the line

And fill them up again!"

Clifford rushes to the pond.

*Glub! Glub!* He must be drinking.

Will Clifford drink the whole pond dry?

That's what some folks are thinking.

But when his giant mouth is full,

He races toward the blaze.

*Swoosh!* Clifford puts the fire out.

Watch the way he sprays!

The fire chief becomes the first

To give the big dog praise.

"I've never seen a better dog

In all my fire-fighting days!"

The folks on Birdwell Island

Begin to realize

That it's wrong to judge a creature

By its color or its size.

Now Clifford is so happy,
As this tale comes to an end.
We love life on Birdwell Island.
Everyone is Clifford's friend.

# BOOKS IN THIS SERIES:

*Welcome to Birdwell Island:* Everyone on Birdwell Island thinks that Clifford is just too big! But when there's an emergency, Clifford The Big Red Dog teaches everyone to have respect—even for those who are different.

*A Puppy to Love:* Emily Elizabeth's birthday wish comes true: She gets a puppy to love! And with her love and kindness, Clifford The Small Red Puppy becomes Clifford The Big Red Dog!

*The Big Sleep Over:* Clifford has to spend his first night without Emily Elizabeth. When he has trouble falling asleep, his Birdwell Island friends work together to make sure that he—and everyone else—gets a good night's sleep.

*No Dogs Allowed:* No dogs in Birdwell Island Park? That's what Mr. Bleakman says—before he realizes that sharing the park with dogs is much more fun.

*An Itchy Day:* Clifford has an itchy patch! He's afraid to go to the vet, so he tries to hide his scratching from Emily Elizabeth. But Clifford soon realizes that it's better to be truthful and trust the person he loves most—Emily Elizabeth.

*The Doggy Detectives:* Oh, no! Emily Elizabeth is accused of stealing Jetta's gold medal—and then her shiny mirror! But her dear Clifford never doubts her innocence and, with his fellow doggy detectives, finds the real thief.

*Follow the Leader:* While playing follow-the-leader with Clifford and T-Bone, Cleo learns that playing fair is the best way to play!

*The Big Red Mess:* Clifford tries to stay clean for the Dog of the Year contest, but he ends up becoming a big red mess! However, when Clifford helps the judge reach the shore safely, he finds that he doesn't need to stay clean to be the Dog of the Year.

*The Big Surprise:* Poor Clifford. It's his birthday, but none of his friends will play with him. Maybe it's because they're all busy. . . planning his surprise party!

*The Wild Ice Cream Machine:* Charley and Emily Elizabeth decide to work the ice cream machine themselves. Things go smoothly. . . until the lever gets stuck and they find themselves knee-deep in ice cream!

*Dogs and Cats:* Can dogs and cats be friends? Clifford, T-Bone, and Cleo don't think so. But they have a change of heart after they help two lost kittens find their mother.

*The Magic Ball:* Emily Elizabeth trusts Clifford to deliver a package to the post office, but he opens it and breaks the gift inside. Clifford tries to hide his blunder, but Emily Elizabeth appreciates honesty and understands that accidents happen.